WEST VIRGINIA

For more information, please contact:
Mascot Books
560 Herndon Parkway #120
Herndon, VA 20170
info@mascotbooks.com

CPSIA Code: PRT1112A
ISBN: 1620860503
ISBN-13: 9781620860502

Printed in the United States

Let's Go Mountaineers!™

Naren Aryal

Illustrated by
Dave D'Incau Jr.

It was a beautiful fall day at West Virginia University. Mountaineer, the university's friendly mascot, was exploring campus on his way to the football stadium.

Two students were walking by Life Sciences and said, "Hello, Mountaineer!" The mascot was happy to see them. Mountaineer wished he had a friend to walk around campus with him. He was feeling a little lonely.

Mountaineer's next stop was the Mountainlair. He hoped that he could find a friend there. The mascot walked to the turf behind the Lair and couldn't believe his eyes! Sitting there before him was a cute dog wearing a coonskin cap. His tail was wagging with excitement!

Mountaineer knew, just by looking at the dog, that he belonged at West Virginia University. Even his name, Musket, was familiar to Mountaineer! Mountaineer decided to show his new best friend all the great things they could do together on campus.

The mascot brought Musket inside the Mountainlair for some bowling! When he walked in, the bowlers greeted him with, "Let's Go Mountaineers!" At first, Musket was a little nervous. He wondered if he could even bowl with paws.

A little girl was there with her parents who attended WVU. She saw that Musket was confused and showed him how to push the bowling ball with his nose. Musket got a strike! Mountaineer was very proud of his new best friend.

Mountaineer knew that the Personal Rapid Transit system was unique to WVU's campus. The PRT carries people all around the school and Morgantown.

Musket loved riding in the electric, computer-driven cars! He couldn't believe how fast they got to their stop. When they got off the PRT, their fellow passengers yelled, "Let's Go Mountaineers!"

Mountaineer and Musket rode the PRT to the Coliseum. Many WVU athletic teams practice at the Coliseum. They went inside to explore some more.

Mountaineer introduced the gymnasts to Musket.
They were happy to meet him and as the two left the
Coliseum, the gymnasts called, "Let's Go Mountaineers!"

Next, Mountaineer brought Musket to see Dick Dlesk Soccer Stadium. While they were running on the bright green grass, the women's soccer coach came over to say hello.

She welcomed Musket into the West Virginia family. As she walked away, she called, "Let's Go Mountaineers!"

Mountaineer and Musket arrived at Milan Puskar Stadium - home of the Mountaineers' football team.

WVU fans were excited for the football game and happy to meet their favorite mascot and his new friend. Fans wearing gold and blue cheered, "Let's Go Mountaineers!"

As the team emerged from the locker room, players cheered, "Let's Go Mountaineers! Go, WVU!"

Musket watched the game from the sidelines and cheered for the home team. He wanted to fetch the football, but decided that wasn't a good idea!

At halftime, The Pride of West Virginia performed the school's fight song. One half of the fans cheered, "Let's Go…!" and the other half replied, "Mountaineers!"

The football team played hard and beat their rivals! The players and coaches celebrated the victory!

Mountaineer gave players high-fives. Musket gave them high-threes because he only has three toes on each paw. Everyone cheered, "Great win, Mountaineers!"

West Virginia University fans were thrilled with the big win. As the two mascots left the stadium, fans called, "See you at the next game!"

After the game, Mountaineer and Musket headed back to the Mountainlair to relax.

They got in a quick game of fetch and Musket knew he was exactly where he belonged. Mountaineer was very happy that he found a new friend and didn't feel lonely anymore.

™

Have a book idea?

Contact us at:

Mascot Books

560 Herndon Parkway

Suite 120

Herndon, VA

info@mascotbooks.com | www.mascotbooks.com

WEST VIRGINIA®